W9-ALW-201

THE SECRET WORLD OF TEDDY BEARS

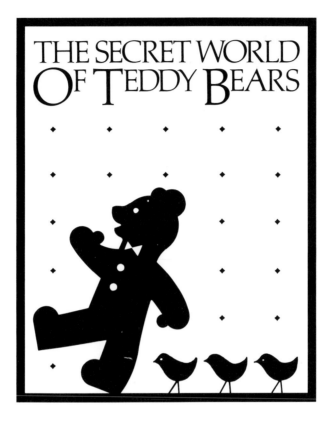

THE SECRET WORLD OF TEDDY BEARS

◆

◆

A rare and privileged
glimpse into the lives they lead
when you're not there.

◆

Written by Pamela Prince
Photographs by
Elaine Faris Keenan
Illustrated and designed by
The Office of
Michael Manwaring

Harmony Books/New York

◆

Published by Harmony Books, a division
of Crown Publishers, Inc.,
One Park Avenue, New York, New York 10016
and simultaneously in Canada
by General Publishing Company Limited

HARMONY and colophon
are trademarks of Crown Publishers, Inc.

Manufactured in Japan.

◆

Library of Congress
Cataloging in Publication Data

Prince, Pamela.
The secret world of teddy bears.

Summary: Poems and photographs
reveal what teddy bears do when humans
aren't around.

1. Teddy bears—Juvenile poetry.
2. Children's poetry, American.
(1. Teddy bears—Poetry. 2. Toys—Poetry.
3. American Poetry.)
1. Keenan, Elaine Faris, ill.
II. Title.

PR3566.R57354 1983 811'.54 83–27

ISBN: 0-517-55022-9

◆

10 9 8 7 6 5 4 3

First Edition

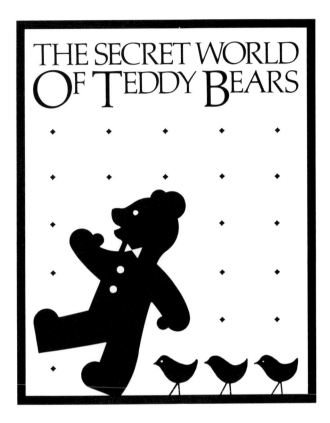

THE SECRET WORLD OF TEDDY BEARS

A secret world of fantasy
is what we'd like to share
with all of you and all your friends
and with *your* Teddy Bear.

Some say that dolls don't spring to life
but, come now, that's not right!
Why, don't you hear those whispers
from the toy box late at night?

They play and sing and dance and dream
and laugh and cry; it's true.
It's just that usually their land
is hidden from our view.

Now in this book and through these pages
you will come to see
that magic and enchantment
are as real as you and me.

And next time when you go to hold
your favorite Teddy Bear,
please treat him with an extra bit
of love, respect and care.

BRENDA poses at the bar.
"Someday I shall be a star,"
muses she, "a pirouette,
in my tutu of pink net:
light as a feather, soft as air.
Oh, never has there been a bear
like me," says she with simple charm,
with a sylphlike wave of a furry arm.

Brenda at the practice bar

ARCEL'S an even-tempered cub;

he seldom is a brat.
As long as he's taken each morning at ten
for a stroll in his pram with his hat,
and his bottle filled up with fresh honey,
and as long as the weather is sunny,
and if all the soft pillows are plumped up just right,
and his favorite blanket is tucked in so tight
near his toes as he likes it, well, then rest assured
that nothing but gurgles and coos will be heard.

But if for some reason
it's the rainy season,
or if there's no honey in store,
or if his fine buggy
is not quite so snug, he
will let out a terrible roar.
He fusses, he screams,
oh, he makes awful scenes;
you just wouldn't believe all his howling.
For such a small bear
he can stir up a scare
with his whimpering, crying, and growling!

*Marcel enjoys a
sunny day from the comfort
of his pillowed pram*

SUZETTE makes up her furry face,
surrounded by ribbons and satins and lace.
Tonight is the night she's been dreaming of,
for she thinks she has found a boy bear she can love,
and this evening he's asked her to go on a date,
so she's primping in hopes that she'll fascinate.

She's put three dabs of perfume behind her right ear
and has checked how she looks sixteen times in the mirror.
Her nose has been powdered, her coat softly brushed,
and a touch of red rouge makes her cheeks pinkly blushed.
"Oh, what more can I do? I'll just sit here and wait."
And the door bell rings promptly at quarter to eight.

Suzette primps in anticipation
of an enchanted evening

U PON the veranda
(with graceful bear features)
is lovely Amanda
and four tiny creatures.
Kitty-Kat sits nestled under her arm,
and the three peppy pups want to show off their charm,
for today they are having their photograph taken.
"Stop fussin', stop wigglin', stop jigglin', and shakin',"
Amanda keeps telling the squirming quartet,
"for you've got to be still; if you're not, I will bet
that instead of a portrait that shows off our fur,
our faces, and eyes, it will all be a blur!"
So the five held their breath, and they counted to three,
and the camera clicked...and got just what you see.

Amanda asks her friends
to stop squirming

BRUNO Bakerman

rolls his pin
to ready the pies
and put them in
the oven to bake,
so he can munch
some savory ones
in time for lunch.

Pumpkin, pecan,
apple, and cherry
custard and mincemeat,
and one huckleberry;
chocolate creams
and strawberry tarts
that are made in the shape
of red Valentine hearts.

(If you can stop by
around about two,
Bruno will have a pie
waiting for you.)

Bruno Bakerman bakes some pies

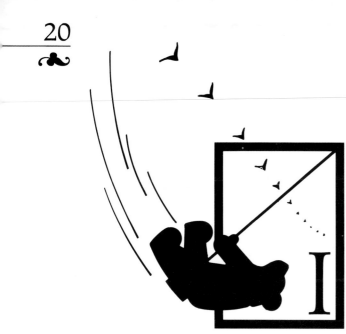

I N blossoming branches rich with flowers

Sylvia swings for hours and hours.
She hums to herself while the birds chirp and fly,
and together they sail way up to the sky,
and back down to the earth and then up once again
and then down and then up until the moment when
her head's in a spinning and rapturous whirl
and she knows that she's one dizzy Teddy Bear girl.
"Time to rest, catch my breath, straighten up my pink bow,
and savor this sweet Springtime's afternoon glow."

SIMON studies every night,
reading by the candlelight.
He knows more than most bears do:
that Columbus sailed the ocean blue,
that one and one indeed make two,
and who won the Battle of Waterloo.

But facts can get so dull, it seems.
Most times he far prefers the dreams,
ideas, and all the other things
inside of books, like queens and kings,
and strange fine lands and golden rings,
and bright new thoughts each volume brings.

When college comes, he's sure to be ready,
for he's an educated Teddy.
He knows about algebra, history, and art,
and he's learned how to think with his mind and his heart.

Simon studies
into the wee hours

JULIA daydreams all the time.
Her head's up in a cloud.
At school her teacher has to shout
and speak to her quite loud.
"Oh, Julia dear, my little friend,
I see you here today,
but I suspect your mind and thoughts
are very faraway!"
And when she's home and in her room,
she thinks of being out,
and when she's out, she ponders
what it's like inside, no doubt.
She's dreaming now of all the things
that she would like to be:
a movie star, a princess
in a silver fantasy,
a heroine upon a horse,
the toast of all the town,
an opera singer, famed and rich,
of worldwide renown.

Julia has a difficult time
paying attention because she's
always daydreaming

E hasn't been new in quite a while,
but Monroe's got a lot of style.
Today he's asked his Kitty-Kat
and favorite Aunt to come and chat,
and share some thoughtful conversation
in a spirit of mutual admiration.
"I've seen a lot of life, you know;
my fur is worn and tattered.
When I look back upon the past,
it's friendships that have mattered.
So here's a toast to both of you;
I'm really glad you're here.
I hope you'll come back very soon....
More tea, Cecilia, dear?"

Monroe is a gracious and
genteel host to his
Aunt Cecilia and Kitty-Kat

THE meadow's green, the flowers sweet,
and we have many good things to eat.
Ah, what a day! What lovely air!
How nice to be a Teddy Bear!

We brought some chums: our little Dog,
and Hoppity Rabbit, and George the Frog.
There's always enough for us to share!
How great to be a Teddy Bear!

Pass the bread and pass the cheese.
Be sure to taste the chicken, please.
Have an apple, plum, or pear!
Such fun to be a Teddy Bear!

Bert's got on his sailor shirt,
and Mae and Sue look awfully pert
in matching hats! I say! Such flair!
How fine to be a Teddy Bear!

"This afternoon I shall recall
for all my life," says Tiz to Paul.
"A perfect time without a care!"
How grand to be a Teddy Bear!

Tizzie Bear and Paul pick flowers
on a perfect picnic day

RANKLIN'S feeling sick today.

His Mom won't let him out to play.
"Take it easy! Don't get up!
Just stay in bed and pet the pup!"

"I wonder why I feel so bad?
Could it be the sweets I've had?
Could it be the seven cakes
I ate at lunch?" (His tummy aches.)
"Or could it be the chocolate pie
I had for breakfast? My, oh, my,
perhaps it was the sugar tart
I gobbled from Grandma's pastry cart
after drinking soda pop
with cherries floating on the top.
I took some cookies from the jar
but only six 'cause the candy bar
was right nearby; and now I'm ill.
I *certainly* have had my fill.

*Franklin is not
feeling his best today*

MELIA went to tea one day.

She met a birdie on the way.

"Won't you join me," was her query,

"for jam and crumpets, perhaps some sherry?

We'll soon become friends — we can sit, we can talk.

And, if you would like, we can go for a walk.

I've brought some nice cookies; we'll nibble a sweet.

Oh, please say you'll share a fine sugary treat

or anything else that you might care to eat."

And the little bird nodded her head, and said, "Tweet!"

*Amelia and the little
yellow bird get acquainted*

M

R. Winfield Bearington

is good at making money.
He's the owner of a firm
that packages fresh honey.
He sends the energetic cubs
into the woods to see
and talk with nearly
seven hundred sixty thousand bees.
They give the honey that they make
to all these busy bears,
who take it back to Bearington,
who samples all the wares.
He personally will taste each batch
and only sells the best,
and that is why he's rich enough
to sport silk tie and vest.

Mr. Winfield Bearington III
begins a busy day at the office

HOWARD used to be quite tubby,
roly-poly, chunky, chubby.
Late last March he started running
and see him now! So trim! So stunning!
He rises at six and goes out to jog
at least five miles with Rudy, his dog,
and they huff and they puff through the neighborhood.
"It's worth it, though, to look this good!"
he thinks as he glances with pride at his thighs.
"Hmmm, still somewhat pudgy…" he notes and he sighs.
But he doesn't slacken his pace, not one bit,
for this is a bear who's not willing to quit
till he's in perfect shape, muscled, and fit.

*Howard is a firm believer in
running five miles a day*

LL the bears sit very still
as Ben begins and reads
of lovely maidens and a Prince
and of his gallant deeds,
of magic woods and Unicorns
in far-off foreign lands,
of villains, too, and witches,
who concoct some nasty plans.
His tales cast enchanted spells
upon the listening toys.
It's not so different, really,
when you read to girls and boys.

Benjamin Bear recounts
an enchanted fairy tale to
the reading circle

LÉLIA dreams of Parisian cafés,
of poodles, perfumes, and the Champs-Elysées.
This morning she learned how to say *s'il vous plait*,
and yearns for a fling with Maurice Chevalier,
who would appreciate her and her romantic air,
who would see in her more than a Teddy Bear,
who would see in her all that is wondrous and rare,
a creature most splendid, enchanting, and fair.

Lélia dreams of Parisian cafés

FREDDIE rides in special style
when he goes into town.
He perches on a nifty seat
of soft white fluffy down.
A built-in horn that can be honked
is another pleasant feature
of traveling upon the back
of this fine-feathered creature.
"I love to journey with my friend;
I think it can't be beat.
Who needs a train or bus or car
when he's got two webbed feet?"

Little Cub Fred and
Jack the Duck set off to pay
some social calls